# Giving Him More To Love
## A BBW Romance

Shaneeka Porter

## Chapter I: Mr. Wiggles

"Beep, beep, beep, beep…" The horrendous sound of the loud alarm goes off and wakes Keisha out of a deep sleep. Her dark brown eyes pop open as she reaches over to turn off the screeching alarm on her phone. *"Another day another dollar"*, she thinks to herself as all the crap she has to do today goes through her mind. That stupid alarm had just waken her up out of her wonderful dream. She was dreaming of a dark chocolate powerful man with greasy big muscles that was licking whipped cream off her size DD breasts. There was nothing Keisha liked more than getting between the sheets with a fine gentlemen, but she understood that every man was not confident enough to handle her curves. Keisha is a brick house; she's super thick and she embraces every single thing about her voluptuous body. People, mainly smaller women, tend to have a lot of assumptions about heavier women: such as they're not healthy, that they don't take care of themselves, and that all of them have low self-esteem. But Keisha managed to rise above the haters that told her that she was anything less than beautiful. Before she could sit up in her bed

Wiggles came running in like a big ball of energy and began licking the bottom of her chin.

"Good morning baby!" she said to her dog. "Today is going to be great, it's my last day on Earth working for someone else."

Keisha has her own hair styling business that she's going to pursue full time; she has built up enough clientele over the last few years in order to leave her day job at the Library. And tonight she will celebrate, but the first thing she has to do is take Wiggles for his morning walk. Keisha sits on the edge of her fluffy bed and lifts her arms up while stretching and yawning as Wiggles runs around her feet, jumping up and down and barking; he's ready to be fed. She ignores Wiggles because he already knows her morning routine, she'll feed him after she uses the bathroom and brushes her teeth. She sleepily strolls into the bathroom and looks at her reflection in the mirror. As she looks into her own deep brown eyes she sees a strong black woman who can do anything she sets her mind to.

Keisha was always a thicker girl, but she never had low self-esteem. Back in college she would talk to all the little skinny girl's men, and they never understood what they were doing wrong; but she always knew it to be true that men like to have a little bit more to hold on to. Her curves were impossible to ignore, and if she walked pass any man, he's bound to break his neck looking at her fat ass and big breasts. She finally finishes brushing her teeth and moves the clear curtains aside to turn on the shower. She places her pink glittery nails under the running water to test its temperature, it's not ready yet, so she runs in the kitchen to feed Wiggles. She returns back to the bathroom, the bottom of her feet slaps against the cold tile floor as she walks over to the shower. Her mint night gown hits the floor and she steps into the hot running shower. While lathering up her luffa with cucumber melon soap, she can hear Mrs. Hall from downstairs arguing with her husband again…"*Uggh, I can't wait to get out of this small ass apartment*" she thinks to herself. Her chocolate silver dollar nipples begin to harden as the water beats against her soft delicate skin. She begins to wash her body slowly, enjoying pressure of the water a little more than she should. She began to think back to her dream, she could really use some dick-- it's been a while since she's been with anyone. As she thinks about a nice chocolate man with huge muscles and six pack abs she begins to squeeze the tip of her nipples. A streak of pleasure runs through her and her clit begins to pulsate letting her know that her pussy is getting wet. One of her hands slide down slowly to her box and she begins to move the tip of her fingers slowly in a circular motion. She widens her legs in order to get more access to her throbbing clit, one of her hands still pinching her nipple. Her head tilts back in ecstasy as she explodes right onto her fingers. She feels much better now, much more relaxed, her shower continues and she steps out to get ready for her day.

Lowland park is only two blocks away from her house, Keisha loves walking Wiggles there because there's a long circular trail to walk on. The sun beats down on her shoulders as she holds Wiggles leash. Wiggles stops to go to the bathroom, and she is interrupted by a guy's voice...

"Hey... sorry to bother you, but you dropped this," said Adrian.

Before Keisha could respond, Wiggles begin barking at the strange man and goes on to try and bite at his legs. Adrian quickly takes a few steps back while laughing a little... "Whoa! I think he likes me."

Keisha laughs and can't help but notice how fine this brother is that's standing right in front of her. He towered over her, he was probably about 6"4, and his big muscular arms popped out of his tank top exposing that he's no stranger to the gym.

"He's usually friendly," Keisha says shyly as she picks up Wiggles to ensure he doesn't try and bite Adrian again. It's crazy because Wiggles is friendly and usually likes everyone.

"Hmmm…maybe there's something about me that he finds intimidating," Adrian replies, smiling ear to ear. "Anyway, I was stopping you to tell you that you dropped this," Adrian handed Keisha her headphones. She's not surprised because she's always losing these small things—she hates the ones that go in your ear anyways because they feel uncomfortable and keep coming out.

"Thank you," Keisha replies, she can't help but feel a little uncomfortable talking to this sexy man. "I'm always losing these things."

"Yeah it happens! I'm just happy your dog calmed down," Adrian said, stepping closer to Keisha since Mr. Wiggles went on to smell the grass a few inches away.

Keisha laughs nervously and finally gets the courage to say "You must be special, because I've never seen him act like this. Take it as a compliment." Keisha is never aggressive with men, she lets them approach her and flirt with her, but she wants Adrian to understand that she's into him.

"Well that's great then," Adrian said smiling. "I'm Adrian by the way," he says as he holds out his hand for a hand shake.

Keisha quickly grabs his hand and introduces herself also, "I'm Keisha, nice to meet you."

"You're beautiful Keisha, can I take you out sometime; or do you already have a special someone?"

"No one special yet, sure... I'd love to go out," Keisha accepted quickly. She didn't enjoy playing games.

When it came to men she liked to be direct and let them know exactly what she's feeling and thinking at any given time.

"Okay, let me have your number," Adrian says with his hand out, expecting Keisha to hand him her phone.

Keisha hands her phone over happily. As he looks down to enter his number in her phone and she tells him hers, she has a high feeling. She can't believe this day is starting off so well.

"I'll be calling you. Make sure you pick up. But I'll let you go for now, you probably have to get to work, right?" Adrian says.

"Yup, I work right at the library on Cherry Street."

"Oh okay, I've been in there a few times. Let me stop running my mouth. I'll talk to you soon," says Adrian, going in for a hug.

Keisha hugs him back and they go their separate ways. Keisha finishes walking Mr. Wiggles and heads to work. All day at work her head spins as she thinks about the perfect encounter she had with Adrian. Thanks to Mr. Wiggles, it made everything so much more fun and interesting. She stares at her phone, making sure she doesn't miss a call from this man, he promised to call her and she's pretty sure he will.

He had to feel the same connection she did, it was an amazing encounter that she'd never forget. Keisha went around the library and collected stray books as she thought about what he did for a living, she never got to ask him that. And she didn't get to check out what he was driving because they went in opposite directions. All the questions stirred in her head. She wondered what day they would go on the date and where he would take her. Her whole workday passed and she still was excited about this new adventure she was about to embark. She hurried home, she didn't want to be stuck in the car if he called.

Keisha walked in the door after a long day's work and plopped on the coach. She turned on the TV as she walked over to the kitchen to make her a sandwich. She made sure the volume of her phone was on high, so she could hear if Adrian called. She ate her lunch meat sandwich with some chips on the side and dozed off while watching reality TV. She awoke suddenly to her phone ringing.

"Hello...?" Keisha answered. She got up on her feet and tried to shake the tiredness out of her voice. She was hoping the call was from Adrian.

"Hey, this is Adrian. We met at the park this morning."

"Hey Adrian, it's nice to hear from you."

"Nice to hear from you too. So, what are you up to?"

"Nothing much, about to get dinner started then take Mr. Wiggles out for his evening walk."

"That's sounds fun."

"Eeeh, it's okay," she said giggling. "What are you up to?"

"Just hit the gym. Now I'm about to go to practice with the team."

"Oh, you play a sport?"

"Yup, I'm a pro football player. That won't be a problem, will it?"

"Of course not. It'll be interesting, I never really watched any football games before."

"Really? That's crazy! You have to come to my next game. My next home game is next week. I'll get you two tickets just in case you want to bring a friend."

"Wow! I'd like that. Thank you!"

"No problem. So… about this date. How does tomorrow night sound?"

"It sounds perfect. How should I dress?"

"Dress fancy because I'm taking you to a nice restaurant."

"Okay, sounds great! I look forward to it," Keisha heart is pounding out of her chest. Ever since she found out Adrian is a football player she's been nervous that she'd say the wrong thing and mess everything up. She really hit the jackpot this time! She can't believe she may be landing a football player, the thought of it seems foreign to her. Like it's out of her league. She's dated her share of wealthy men, but never anyone like this. She has to be on point at all times, there's no way she's going to let this one slip through her fingers.

"As do I, I'll talk to you later, beautiful."

As soon as the phone hangs up Keisha jumps up and down in excitement. Her heart beats fast and she can't believe that such a great man wants to get to know her better. She begins dancing around her small efficient apartment as Mr. Wiggles runs between her feet, getting excited along with her. She eventually tires herself out and plops back on the coach, still smiling ear to ear. She calls her best friend Melanie to tell her what's going on.

"Hello?" Melanie says as she picks up the phone. You can hear the open road behind her, for she is just getting off work and is stuck in traffic once again.

"Hey girl… wassup with you? Are you busy?"

"Not really, in traffic again… wassup? How was your last day of work?" asks Melanie. Trying to get her mind off being angry about the traffic.

"It was boring as usual. But the rest of my day wasn't."

"And why is that?"

"I met a guy… a professional football player and we're going out on a date tomorrow night a fancy expensive restaurant."

"Wow! You go girl," Melanie says, being a little bit jealous. Not only is Keisha able to quit her job, but she also meets a rich guy. She wonders to herself when her breakthrough will come.

"Thanks girl. You should stop by and have a glass of wine with me, I want to tell you the whole story."

"Girl I would but it's late and I have work in the morning, but I'll definitely catch you on Thursday at my hair appointment."

"Oh okay, that's fine. The story is not that deep anyways, basically Mr. Wiggles attacked him and he returned my headphones I had dropped and asked me out."

"Where were you at? Walking in the park?"

"Yup, I was walking Wiggles as usual and everything happened just like that."


"Things are really turning around for you, I'm happy for you," Melanie lied. She wished it was her in that park, and she wishes it was her quitting her job. She didn't understand how this fat bitch could be so lucky. She took care of herself and her appearance, and yet, she's still working a minimum wage job and can't find a rich man to marry. That's her plan, to marry rich. That's why she works so hard in the gym, eats right, and always keeps her hair and nails done. So she could have a rich man come and save her from the day to day grind. But she smiles as she thinks about what Keisha's situation can mean for her, she can be introduced to one of his team mates. So she decides to play it cool with Keisha, and really be invested in anything she's doing so she can make her move and find her a pro ball player too.

"Thanks girl, I know your time will come too. God has everything planned out for us both. All we can do is live our best lives and make the most of each moment," said Keisha, happy that her friend Melanie was complimenting her. She usually didn't do that. Melanie is Keisha's closest friend, but Keisha knows Melanie can get kind of jealous at times. She's always trying to take the spotlight and thinks everything is all about her.

"Yeah I hope so. I'm hoping God will send me a rich man who will take me out of this day to do bullshit. I'm just tired. I look too good to work so hard."

"In time you'll get exactly what you deserve," Keisha said, meaning every word.

"Thanks girl, anyway, let me get off this phone. This girl in the next car over keeps giving me the evil eye. I guess she's mad she doesn't have anyone to talk to while she's in traffic. She needs to be paying attention to her two kids in the back seat and stop looking over here," Melanie said, rolling her eyes at the white lady in the next car over and pulling out the mirror in her purse to apply a fresh coat of lipstick.

"Girl… you're something else," Keisha said laughing. "Alright, I'll see you Thursday. Have a great day and I hope you get out of traffic soon."

"Exactly. Before I hurt somebody!" Melanie said, hanging up the phone.

## Chapter II: Date Night

Keisha was dressed and ready to go. She had on a form fitting black dress that had a lot of lace in the front and showed a large portion of her back. She finished off her stunning outfit with gold heels and jewelry. When she walked pass the full length body mirror she did a full turn to admire her many curves. She smiled as she thought to herself *"My curves give me courage."* Getting a date with Adrian simply reinforced the idea that you don't have to be small to get a man. Some men like more to love, and she wouldn't be holding anything back tonight. Keisha skipped into the bathroom and sprayed some of her finest perfume all over her body, she was now ready to go. All she had to do was wait for the call. She looked out her window and saw the streets were bare and everyone was most likely inside on this fine Wednesday night spending time with their loved ones. She didn't live on a busy street and she was thankful for that, because she loves her peace and quiet. But that doesn't matter much because her neighbors are always super loud, her apartment walls are super thin and you can hear everything going on—things you'd prefer living your whole life without hearing. As she stood in the window seal, she saw her phone begin to light up and then her ringtone alerted her that her night was about to begin.

She came outside and saw a black Cadillac out front; Adrian stepped out of the car, looking fine as hell and opened the passenger door for Keisha. Before she stepped into the car, they hugged. She saw that he was dressed in a tux, and she was very impressed and excited for what lied ahead for her.

"You smell amazing, are you ready for tonight?" Adrian said, smiling and helping her get in. Adrian walked around and got in the driver's seat awaiting Keisha's response.

"Thanks, you're such a gentlemen. I'm absolutely ready for tonight." Keisha couldn't believe this was happening. She didn't care what happened after tonight, just this experience was going to be something to treasure.

The two drove off into the night, ready for adventure and great food. As Keisha stepped out of the car she could feel a hint of cold breeze hit her face. It was fall, and she was beginning to think winter was coming early. As she stepped out the car, she could hear music coming from the festive block. There were shining lights, music, and people everywhere smiling, laughing and enjoying their time. As they walked the crowded streets, Keisha realized that she'd never been to this part of town before. How could she live so close and not have heard of this place. As she did more research in her mind, she could see that everyone was dressed in expensive clothes. The men had on fancy watches, and the women had on designer hand bags. She realized she'd never been there because these people were rich, she had never hanged with the wealthy before. It was definitely something new. All her friends and family were either struggling financially, or just getting by. This was going to be one hell of a night!

As they approached, Keisha could see now that this restaurant will be unlike anything she'd ever experienced. There were intricate designs on the tall glass doors and the door handles looked like they were made of gold. As Adrian pulled open one of the heavy glass doors, Keisha entered to see people dressed in tuxedos and fancy gowns. The waiters and waitresses were even dressed up, holding shiny silver platters full of food and drinks over their heads. Keisha had never seen anything so classy in her life. She felt a little out of place. Adrian approached the counter and she couldn't hear what him and the greeter discussed, all she knew is he grabbed her hand and they started walking through the restaurant and ended up at a table for two.

Keisha sat across from Adrian on the fancy wooden detailed chairs and glanced slowly at the beautiful place settings. Then she glanced back up at Adrian and smiled.

"Thanks for everything, I'm having a great time already," said Keisha.

"No problem, tonight is going to be really fun. You told me some things about you on the ride over, but I'd love to know more," Adrian replied.

"Well…, you already know that yesterday was my last day working at the library. I'm going to pursue my hair businesses full time. I'm 32 and I don't have any kids yet, just a crazy dog. And I enjoy reading and cooking. Is there anything specific you want to know?"

"Yes, actually there is. How is a beautiful woman like you still single?"

Keisha blushed. And a big lump took over her throat, making her too shy to speak.

"You're successful, sexy, and you seem like you're not crazy. So why are you single?" Adrian continued, excited to hear her reply.

Keisha finally go the courage to speak up, "I'm not sure why I'm single. I know it may sound cliché, but I guess I haven't met the right guy yet..."

"Well, I'm not going to put you on the spot anymore because I'm happy you're not taken. That just means I get to know you better and see how far we can go."

"Thanks. I'm excited to get to know you better as well. So, now...tell me about yourself."

"Well, I'm 28 and I grew up in California. I went to college for football, I got drafted and now I play in the leagues to make a long story short. I don't have a sob story where my parents were poor and I overcame adversity. It wasn't easy getting to where I was and I didn't get any handouts. But I'm just not your typical "boy from the hoods manages to be successful despite the odds stacked against him". And I'm single because this lifestyle I live isn't easy. It comes with a lot of sacrifice and travel, and a lot of females are gold diggers and actively look for men with money. I can't stand those types of chicks; I've had my share and I can't deal with someone who isn't loyal. I want to start settling down and really see what love is like."

"Completely understandable. It has to be hard dealing with not knowing who actually likes you as a person and who just wants to get near you because of what you have."

"It is... sorry I'm talking your ear off. Let's order something," Adrian says as he picks up the menu. As soon as the menu is in his hands a waitress comes over and takes the drink orders.

"So what's good here?" Keisha says to Adrian looking at the menu confused.

"I like the filet mignon, it's delicious."

"Hmm... I'll have that then." Keisha is sort of confused because the menu doesn't even have prices on it. She guesses that if you have to ask how much it is, I guess you shouldn't be buying it.

"You'll love it. I think I'll have it too. Anyways, yeah I'm tired of living the same way. I'm a grown man now, I've had my fun and I'm ready to do something different so I can have something different."

Before Keisha could respond, the blonde waitress came back with their red wine and took the food orders. She was so impressed by the promptness and politeness of the staff here.

"So your hair business, how long have you been building that?" Adrian asks.

"About five years now as an official business. But I've been doing hair since I was a little girl, about twelve years old. So I know a thing or two about hair."

"Really, so do you have male clients as well, like do you know how to do a shape up?"

"I sure do. I only have about three male clients though. They usually go to barber shops."

"Wow, that's really interesting. Congratulations on everything. There's nothing like a woman who knows how to make a pretty penny. I may be a new client of yours..." Adrian laughs.

"Thanks, I truly appreciate that," Keisha responded, feeling like the luckiest girl in the world to be complimented by such a great man.

Before they know it, their dishes are in front of them and it's time to eat. Adrian and Keisha lock eyes and Adrian let's her know the he usually prays over his meal. They take hands and bless the meal. They continue to talk about everything under the sun: business, relationships, future plans, and more. Keisha can't believe how much fun she is having; she cherishes every single moment they spend together. On the way back home, an R&B love song comes on the radio, a song that neither of them have ever heard before. They both listen to the lyrics intensely and Adrian breaks the silence.

"So, how was everything tonight? Did I impress you?" He says, joking with Keisha.

"Very impressive. Thanks again for everything."


"Oh, we're not finished just yet…"


"What else do we have planned?"


"You shall see…"


They continue to ride into the night until they approach a building with jazz music blasting loudly. Adrian parks the car in the back of the building and they walk up to the front entrance. Keisha looks up and sees a tall intimidating security guard with big muscles and a serious face. Before she could step back a little, Adrian puts his hand on the small of her back, nods at the security guard in approval, and the guard opens up the door allowing them to enter. As soon as the door opens, loud music floods their ears. They can see tons of smoke and blue musty lights as they enter the club. As they walk further in, they see the band performing on a low stage, and round tables on the sides, and a wooden dance floor filled with black people clapping their hands and dancing. They were dancing some sort of old school dance that you'd see in the movies from back in the day, Keisha had never seen something like this up close. She was intrigued to say the least. She couldn't help but smile and watch the audience dancing as they approached an empty table to set their stuff down. She looked over at the band once again and saw the men playing their instruments with such passion. They guy with the saxophone had on a straw hat and black sunglasses, you can see the sweat dripping down his face, and every time he blew into the saxophone you can see the veins popping out of his neck. The whole band was up there jammin' and having a great time. The whole club was live. Adrian took Keisha's hand and they headed to the dance floor, *"oh no, I'm not a dancer at all, Keisha though to herself—Lord, please don't let me ruin this..."* Adrian took both of Keisha's hands in his and began moving them back in forth, he started moving his feet and swaying from side to side. She could see that this was not his first time dancing to the jazz music. Keisha attempted to copy the same moves that Adrian was making; he smiled and continued to dance with her. After a few minutes, Adrian left to got to the bar and get them some drinks. After about two more drinks, Keisha didn't care what she looked like out on that dance floor, she was getting loose and having a great time. She and Adrian danced the night away.

Keisha stepped out of the car, it was already getting light outside, she looked at her phone and couldn't believe that they'd stayed out partying until 4:30 in the morning; she was exhausted. Adrian walked her to her door and they looked each other in the eyes as they stood in the doorway. Adrian leaned over and gave Keisha a gentle peck on the lips.

"Goodnight, my beautiful black queen," he said with confidence.

"Goodnight, thanks for everything. I can't remember the last time I had so much fun."

"You're welcome. Get some rest. I know you have a hair to do in about three hours."

Keisha smiled at Adrian in understanding, then turned around and walked into her apartment feeling like a million bucks. She flopped on her bed and set her alarm for 8AM. She knew she wouldn't get much rest, but she was so happy she didn't care. She dozed off immediately with thoughts of happily ever after in her mind.

## Chapter III: Ain't None of Your Friend's Business

Adrian heads to practice, his head is still pounding from lasts night's festivities. He's so happy to have found a woman like Keisha. He plans to give her his all, he loves everything about her so far. He prayed day in and day out for God to send him a great woman. And when they met in the park, he could see in her eyes that she was genuine and well rounded.

While speeding down the road, he blasts his rap music while bobbing his head to the beat, he enjoys his rap-- it always pumps him up before practice. *"It's going to be a great practice today, I can't wait to tell the guys about Keisha,"* he thought to himself. As he pulled into the lot at the field, he looked down at his watch to see what time it was. He noticed that the watch was upside down, so he twists it around his caramel arm, the hair from his arm catching in the process. He then jogs slowly inside with his duffle bag beating against his side, he speeds up even more so he won't be late; he wasn't in the mood for the coach to be on his ass this morning.

Adrian arrives in the locker room just in time, and immediately begins to take out his practice gear and begins changing. As he looks around, all his team mates are pretty much already dressed. They're standing around talking about what they've been up to. It's a very tight knit community, they're like brothers who share with everything with each other.

"And then, she had the nerve to get mad. I wasn't even trying to fuck her sister. That bitch is trippin'. I'm getting tired of her. The only reason I'm sticking around is because she got that good good," Mike complains.

Mike is one of Adrian's best friends on the team. He's been in the league for almost six years now so he's like the captain of the team, but not officially. Six years is like two decades when it comes to pro football; so a lot of the guys look up to him for advice with their careers. But they know to stay wary of his relationship advice because he's always in some shit. He can't seem to get it right, he's 36 years old now and has never been married and has no kids. Mike was the one person who really protected Adrian when he first started playing for the team, he took it easy on him and didn't haze him like the other guys. Ever since then, Adrian took a liking to Mike and has been a loyal friend to him.

"You really need to get it together," Adrian said out loud, teasing Mike.

"I know you're not talking, you can't even get to practice on time. Plus, you can't seem to keep a girl yourself," Mike responds, laughing.

"Actually, I met a new girl. We had a good time last night. I took her out to eat and to the jazz club and we really connected," said Adrian.

"And... she's a gold digger right? Did you tell her you play ball?" asked Jimmy, one of the other guys on the team.

"Yes, but not until after I asked her out. I can tell she's not a gold digger, she's different," Mike assured them.

"Look... every woman is a gold digger in their own way. Some are just worse than others in my opinion. They always want something; the days of just liking someone for themselves is over. It's a new day and age. The sooner you realize that the better," said Cornell, another team member.

"I totally disagree," said Mike. "There are some good girls out there. They're just a dying breed. You have to just do your research and see who they've previously dated, if they have their own money, and if they are good in bed... wait... that last one is just simply a requirement," Mike says, making the other guys chuckle.

"That sounds like a lot of work," said Cornell.

"Exactly, I have other things to do. I don't have time to be researching around. That's some chick shit. Guys don't do all that," Jimmy responded, shaking his head.

"Well, I know my girl isn't like that. I don't need any research. She has her own business and she's just a sweetheart," Adrian says, changing the subject and bragging about his new found love.

"Is she sexy?" asked Cornell.

"Yup, she's thick and beautiful," says Adrian.

"Really? How thick. She's not a fat bitch is she?" says Cornell. All the guys in the locker room begin laughing; making Adrian feel uncomfortable with sharing any more information with them. He knew Keisha's a little bigger, but he didn't mind that. He liked how soft she felt when he hugged her, and all her curves.

"Chill. She's not fat. Just thick," Adrian shot back.

"Well we have to meet her. Is she coming to next week's game?" asked Mike.

"I think so, I have to see if she's busy or not," Adrian lied. He didn't want the team to meet Keisha anymore. He didn't want to get clowned for being with a big girl. Keisha already confirmed she could come to the game, but he would have to figure something else out because there's no way he was going to bring her in front of all these shallow assholes. He had a need to protect her and her feelings. There was no way he was going to stop seeing her, he decided then and there to keep his sex life private for now on.

The coach came in yelling at the team for small talking and not being out of the field. It was time for Adrian to get to work.

## Chapter IV: Hiding The Goods

Melanie sits down in Keisha's salon chair, ready to get her hair done. She can't wait for all the details about Keisha's new man. She needs wants to know exactly how everything went down, she has plans to get Keisha to set her up on a double date. Melanie really needs a rich man, she's willing to do anything to find and secure a husband who has money. She doesn't care what he looks like, how many kids he has, or what he does. If he has money, she'll marry him. She understands that she's getting older and her worth is deteriorating; her looks won't last forever and she needs to make things happen soon.

"So how was it? Tell me everything!" Melanie says excitedly.

"Girl... it was everything. I never experienced anything like it," said Keisha, prepping Melanie's hair for a deep condition.

"Keep going…"

"Well. He picked me up in his fancy black Cadillac. He even opened the passenger's side door for me…"

"Was it the newest Cadillac from this year?" Melanie interrupted.

"Girl, I don't know anything about cars!" Keisha said annoyed, "All I know is it was a Caddy."

"Ughh, go on…," Melanie said rolling her eyes.

"Anyway, the first stop we made was at this fancy ass restaurant I'd never been to. I'm mean it was fancy as hell. They had niggas in tuxedos and everything, girl. You should have seen it. I didn't even

know how to pronounce the shit on the menu, but I played it cool."


"So what happened next?"


"Then we went to some jazz club where we danced and drank all

night. At first I was all shy, but after I got a few drinks in me—I

started to loosen up."


"Then what?"


"After that we pretty much just went home. He had an early

practice and I had a client."


"So, have you guys talked since then?"

"Yup, every single day. He's supposed to be giving me tickets to his game this weekend."

"Girl! You have to get me the hook up! And I need to meet some of his football friends too."

"I'll see what I can do. We just start talking, so I don't want to ask him for too much too soon."

"Ughh, come on now..."

"I'll ask if he has any single friends, but I'm not asking him for any extra tickets or anything."

"Okay...first things first," Melanie said excitedly rubbing her hands together and smiling. She had plans to come out on top.

Keisha and Melanie continued to gossip and talk about everything going on with them; Keisha finished Melanie's hair and they decided to watch some reality TV while continuing to catch up.

The sun began to disappear and the shrieks of light that usually hit Keisha's kitchen counter began to fade away, Keisha got up to look out the window to see the city beginning to slow down as night time approached. Melanie went home a few hours ago, now Keisha was relaxing with her laptop looking up new ideas on how to promote her business. As she glared out the window, she heard her cell phone vibrate and looked over her shoulder to see it lighting up and ringing. She ran over to it, thinking in the back of her mind that it just may be Adrian. He calls her every single day, and she wants to make sure not to miss the call.

"I miss you," Adrian says.

"I miss you too, when can we meet up again?"

"How about tonight. You should come over to my place. Are you busy?"

"Nope. Not at all."

"Okay, I'll be there to pick you up in about a half hour. See you soon, beautiful."

Then night sky was filled with gray clouds as rain drops began to fall against Keisha's window. She watched with excitement as Adrian's car pulled up in front of her apartment building. She jogged quickly over to her coat rack and grabbed her black rain coat as her phone vibrated in her jean pocket. She struggled a little as she took the phone out of her thigh hugging jeans and answered Adrian's call.

"I'm outside," Adrian said excitedly.

"I'm coming out now," Keisha said, her heart beating because she was a little shy to see Adrian again. She hung up the phone and made her way down the stairwell.

Keisha walked outside to the car slowly, ensuring that her pumps wouldn't get wet from the rain. When she finally looked up, she saw Adrian standing there tall, handsome, and inviting as usual. He bent down to give her a wet kiss on the cheek and opened the passenger's side door for her. She blushed as she got into the car, feeling like the luckiest woman in the world. As they drove to Adrian's house, they had small talk about what's been going on for the past few days. Keisha happened to bring up Melanie.

"Oh yeah, I forgot to mention. My friend Melanie wanted to know if you knew any single guys. She's a real catch and a great person," asked Keisha. Hoping that she wouldn't turn him off by asking for favors already. But she'd do anything for Melanie, she's her best friend; and she would want Melanie to do the same for her.

"Of course, I work with a bunch of men. They're all looking to for wholesome women. Is she anything like you?"

"Well... sort of. We love a lot of the same shows and we're both pet lovers. She's a working woman with a great head on her shoulders; and very pretty too."

"Hmm... Maybe we should do a double date. My brother is actually looking for a good woman."

"That'll be fun. Yeah, we should do that sometime."

"How about next Friday; my brother Daniel is a chef and Friday is the grand opening of his restaurant."

"Wow! Seems like he's doing big things, she'll really like that."

"Great, I'll call him first thing tomorrow," Adrian smiles as he pulls into his driveway. He has the feeling that he'll be getting lucky tonight. He's been wanting time alone with Keisha ever since they met.

Keisha is impressed by the size of Adrian's estate. She can't believe that one person would need this entire house. It's dark, but she can tell the house is a brown color, Keisha smiles as she thinks about how much the structure of Adrian's house looks like a castle. It's made of stone, and it has a huge yard. She is even more impressed when she goes inside. She walks in to the dimly lit welcome area to see a living room space to the right, and right ahead of them is the kitchen. Then she notices the spiral staircase that she guesses must lead to the second floor.

"Your house is beautiful," she compliments.

"Thanks hun, so what would you like to drink?"

"Whatever you have is fine."

Adrian gestures for her to have a seat in the living room. She makes her way over unsure of which black leather couch to choose. She decided to choose the love seat. She sits down, crossing her legs and patiently awaiting her drink. Adrian returns a few minutes later with two wine glasses with a tinted yellow liquid in them. As Keisha takes a sip, she falls in love with the sweet white wine as it rolls off her tongue in into her throat causing a feeling of relaxation.

"This wine is great!" Keisha interrupts the silence.

"Thank you, so… what type of shows do you like?"

"All kinds, romantic comedies, dramas, scary movies. They're all fun."

"I don't know about no romantic comedies, but I can do a drama," Adrian says as he aims the remote control at the huge flat screen TV. He finds a movie to put on and they begin to watch.

Adrian can't take it anymore. He keeps looking down at Keisha's busty cleavage and can't wait to see what kind of lover she is. He takes his hand and slowly rubs Keisha's thigh. Keisha looks him in the eyes, as he continues to caress her leg. They begin to kiss slowly and passionately. Keisha sucks and bites on the bottom of

Adrian's lip, making his manhood get even stiffer. Her clit begins to throb as Adrian begins to lick and suck the side of her neck slowly. Keisha puts her head back, giving him even more access to her neck as she begins to moan. While sucking her neck, he palms one of her breast, causing Keisha's clit to begin to throb again with excitement. He then kisses down her neck landing on her breasts and begins to lift her dress over her head. He grabs her and unbuckles her bra leaving Keisha's busty breast exposed. Her nipples get hard instantly and Adrian puts one in his mouth and begins the taste it. She moans in pleasure as she grabs his dick and begins to jack him off. He moans along with her, not wanting her to stop. He sits back on the couch as Keisha puts his large dick in her mouth and gently begins to bob her head up and down. He grabs the back of her head, encouraging her not to stop. He then grabs a handful of her ass as she continues to suck his dick. After a while he can't take it anymore and explodes in her mouth. Keisha saddles him and begins to ride his dick. Her walls expand and then tighten with pleasure as his long dick goes in and out of her. He grabs her ass as she continues to ride him, enjoying her curvy body. Her big tits continue to bounce up and down and rub against his chest.

Adrian turns Keisha over and puts her in the doggie style position. As he dick enters her, she moans with delight. Her pussy gets wetter and wetter as he pounds in and out of her, her ass flopping up and down. He enjoys her fat ass as squeezes it as he continues to thrust. Keisha can't take it anymore, she cums all over his dick.

Adrian usually doesn't let women stay over his place, but Keisha is special, and they had a special connection. He can't believe how down to Earth she is, and he's falling hard for her so soon. He just can't get over the fact that his friends thinks he can do better. Her size turns him on, she is one of the best lovers he's ever had and he feels amazing when they're bodies touch. He watches her as she sleeps peacefully in his bedroom. There's no way he's letting her go. He wants the best of both worlds; so his best bet is to keep her from ever meeting his friends. There's no way he's giving up a love this good. He decides he just needs to keep her hidden, but at the same time he wants to announce his love for her to the world.

Adrian lays awake looking at his ceiling as he thinks of ways to tell

her she won't be getting any tickets to his games.

## Chapter V: Meeting Melanie

"Oh my God! That's great," Melanie screamed inside feeling like she just hit the jack pot. She couldn't believe her girl Keisha came through for her so quickly. She thought Keisha would play around to try to keep her down, but here she is telling her that she has a chance to meet up with an entrepreneur who's doing big things.

"Yup, so be ready next week. I'm excited too! We just get each other, we connected on another level last night, it was amazing," Keisha said, her clit tinged a little as she though back to all the romancing her and Adrian did last night.

"Girl, I already have my outfit picked out, quit playin'," said Melanie, "so... what did ya'll do over his house? What did it look like? Give me the details!"

"We started watching this show, but it didn't last long because we ended up making love. It was the best sex I've ever had. He really put it down. His house is huge, and I even stayed a night."

"Really? He let you stay a night... this must be serious. So... how big is his you know what?"

"Dang... you need to know all my business?" Keisha blushed. She knew how Melanie is and she used to her upfront and aggressive questioning.

"It's really big actually, I can't wait to get more of it."

"Wow... girl you's a freak. I just hope his brother is packin' too. This is crazy, I can't believe you're dating a football player, this is a dream come true."

"For who?" Keisha said, laughing. Knowing that Melanie is only being selfish and thinking about herself.

"Girl, you know what I mean. This is great for both of us. Two bad bitches taking over! Just the way it should be," Melanie said, rolling her eyes because she knew she looked ten times better than Keisha, especially naked.

Mr. Wiggles startled Keisha by jumping on her lap and barking in her face. "Girl, let me talk to you later, this dog needs fed. But I'm excited for everything, my life is on top right now. I just don't want this fairy tale to end."

The week goes by pretty quickly, Adrian always has Keisha over and Keisha stays at Adrian's every once in a while. She just can't understand why Adrian won't take her out; she's tired of being in the house. But she knows all of this will change at his brother Daniel's restaurant opening. Keisha and Adrian have been getting to know each other very well, and they're very much in love. Adrian knows he can bring Keisha to the grand opening and introduce her as a friend, he won't hardly know anyone there except his bother anyway. Daniel is non-judgmental and won't care who Adrian is dating. Their parents don't even live in Atlanta, so Adrian knows he won't have to introduce her to too many people. It'll mainly be Daniel's friends and employees.

Sooner than later, Friday rolls around and Keisha is getting dressed to go to the grand opening. She's nervous, she's not sure how many of Adrian's friends she'll be meeting but she wants to make a great first impression. She decided to slip on a dress that's sexy, but not too revealing. As she slips on the dark blue jean dress, it feels smooth against her curves and she feels confident that it'll be appropriate for the event. As she turns around back in forth in the mirror and smooths out the sides of her dress, she hears the doorbell ring; she already knows it's Melanie.

"Hey girl, you look nice!" says Melanie, waiting on a compliment back.

"So do you, very sexy, I love it!" Keisha replies.

Keisha runs back in her room to continue getting ready. She sprays some of her sweet smelling perfume all over her body and touches up her makeup. Then she slides into her shiny black pumps and meets Melanie out on the couch.

"Are you ready for tonight?" Keisha asks.

"Born ready, you can drive because I don't do well with night driving," says Melanie.

They head out into the night to the soon to be *Dan's Diner*. They arrive at the restaurant to find that it's packed outside, and there's people waiting to get in. Keisha and Melanie look at each other in frustration as Keisha begins to search for parking. She texts Adrian, letting him know she's outside and he tells them to come to the front entrance. Keisha blushes as her and Melanie make their way to the front doors, she feels uncomfortable cutting so many people in line. No one says anything to them, they just give them nasty looks. As she gets closer she can see that the place is pretty big and they haven't started letting anyone in yet. She feels a little better because she thought it was packed on the inside as well. As she approaches the front door, she sees Adrian and he opens the door to let them inside. They step inside and to the right of them is Daniel waiting there. Daniel looks similar to his brother, he's tall, brown skinned, with is a big smile and kind eyes.


"She's beautiful," Daniel says, looking directly at Keisha.

Everyone else laughs a little as Adrian tells Daniel that Melanie is actually the one he wanted to introduce him to. Keisha feels amazing that Daniel thought she was the one he was being introduced to. She gains confidence as she plays back in her head how he called her beautiful.

"So... Daniel this is Melanie, Melanie meet Daniel and also meet me because this is also my first time meeting you," Adrian says as he takes Melanie's hand into his giving it a shake.

"It's nice to meet you both," Melanie says, going over to shake Daniels hand as well.

"So what time are you going to start letting these people in?" Keisha asks.

Daniel looks at his watch and says, "In about five minutes."

Daniel gives everyone a quick tour of the restaurant. His employees were back in the kitchen prepping food, everything looked clean and polished. You can tell that he put a lot into building this restaurant. When they finish the tour Daniel finally opens the door and the band begins to start playing, it was a great little gathering; he gave out free appetizer coupons at the door to everyone who attended. The four of them, Melanie, Daniel, Keisha, and Adrian stood and a group with drinks in hand talking about work and about how big of an accomplishment it is to open a restaurant. Daniel soon went off to mingle with is other guests, but he made sure to give Melanie his phone number so they can meet again. This was not the date that Keisha had expected, but it was better than sitting in the house all day. She liked that she could be on Adrian's arm without a fuss and show all these people that this fine man was hers. Keisha, Adrian, and Melanie sat down at one of the tables; they were all hungry and came ready to eat. They ordered their food and got their drinks. Keisha bobbed her head to the music, she was having a great time. She and Melanie excused themselves from the table to go freshen up in the ladies room.

"So, what do you think?" Keisha asked, hoping that Daniel would meet her standards.

"He's okay I guess, but I've been doing some thinking and he probably doesn't have a lot of money. This is only his first restaurant and what if it fails?" said Melanie.

"Girl, don't worry about that. You'll be fine. Just give him a chance."

"Easy for you to say, your man makes millions of dollars a year. I just don't want the short end of the stick. You should ask Adrian if he has any football player friends."

"I'm not going to do that, and plus, it seems like Daniel really likes you."

"Well, I can't tell. He's too busy entertaining his guests."

"He's doing what he has to do. That's business, honey."

"Well, you don't have to ask him. I'll ask him myself."

"Wow---" before Keisha could finish her sentence Melanie was already on her way out the bathroom. She couldn't believe the audacity of her. She looked in the bathroom mirror and move the strands from her bangs out of her face. This would be the last time she did something nice for Melanie, she was really beginning to piss her off.

She returned to the table but didn't get to sit for long before her phone began vibrating in her clutch. She took it out to ignore the call, when she saw it was her landlord calling. She couldn't understand why he'd be calling so late unless it was an emergency. She excused herself from the table to take the call as Melanie and Adrian continued to hold their conversation about the hottest new cars.

"Hello?" Keisha answered, hoping that this would not be an emergency.

"Keisha, this is Mr. Cook, I need you to come home right away, there was a fire in your next door neighbor's apartment!"

"Oh my God, is everyone okay?" she asked, concerned.

"Yes everyone is fine, the fire department is here and they have everything under control for now. But they don't know how much damage it has done to the building yet.

"Wow, okay; I'm on my way now."

Keisha hung up the phone and apologized to Melanie and Adrian that she had to leave so soon. Adrian offered to come with her to ensure everything was okay, but she insisted he stay there and enjoy his brother's big night. He let her know he'd call her later. Keisha drove home crying, hoping to God that Mr. Wiggles would be okay.

## Chapter VI: Behind Your Back

"So what do you see in her?" Melanie asked Adrian, not caring if she came off as nosy.

"I see a lot in her, she's beautiful, successful, and a great person," Adrian replied to Melanie; not really wanting to discuss how he felt insecure about her weight and hiding her from his friends.

"Aww... that's cute. So what do your football friends think about her?" Melanie had an agenda to try and get the truth out of Adrian. She knows for sure she looks way better than Keisha, and she was trying to understand how comfortable he felt about her actual appearance when it comes to her weight.

"They really haven't met her yet, but I'm sure they'll love her," Adrian replies, wishing this girl would just change the subject.

"Why haven't they met her yet? Hasn't she been to a game? You guys have been seeing each other for at least two months now?"

"It's been busy. Excuse me while I call Keisha, I need to see if everything is okay with her," Adrian got up and left the table as he dialed Keisha number. He felt bad for staying at Daniel's event, knowing that Keisha was going through a tragedy right now.

Daniel felt relieved as he hung up the phone with Keisha. Everything seems to be alright but there was slight damage to her apartment. So she would be staying with her parent's until the owners got everything together. He felt better as he went back to the table and sat across the table from Melanie once again, ready to face her and her crazy questions.

"So what's the 411," Melanie asked, genuinely hoping Keisha was okay. Although she wasn't the greatest friend, Melanie loved Keisha like a sister and would be devastated if anything happened to her.

"Everything is fine. Mr. Wiggles is safe. She'll be staying with her parents until everything clears up. I guess she's going to go looking for a new apartment."

"Good. I'm glad everything is okay. But don't think you're off the hook. So… what's the real reason you haven't showed off Keisha to your friends. We're all busy, but we make time for the ones we want to show off."

Adrian laughed at Melanie's comment and didn't say a word. He just took another sip of his drink and began to look around the restaurant to see how his brother was doing. By this time it was jammed packed and he could tell that it would be a great success.

He wasn't afraid of Melanie, but her questions were starting to get annoying. He didn't owe her any explanations and she wasn't going to get anything he didn't give her.

"Okay I quit. I just want to make sure my friend is protected, that's all. If you're embarrassed by her just admit it," Melanie said breaking the silence.

"Look... I think she's beautiful, but let's just put it this way. She's not the typical type of girl that any me or my friends would date. I just don't want them to judge me or her before they get to know her. I'll bring her around when I know the time is right."

"The time may never be right. Why not stop wasting your time and get with someone on your level?" Melanie asked, sitting up a little straighter to see if Adrian would notice her cleavage.

"Uggh, you're brutally honest aren't you? I respect that. But it's not as easy as it seems. I actually have feelings for her or I would have stopped talking to her a long time ago. She has everything I like and love, the fucked up thing about it is she's not going to fit into my circle of friends. I wish things could be so perfect."

"Well… did you even tell your friends you had a girl?"

"Yes, and they've been dying to meet her. I wish I hadn't mentioned it, because they're the ones who made me feel insecure about bringing her around. I just don't know what to do at this point."

"It sounds like to me you have two options, get over you fear of what people think of you and introduce Keisha to your friends, or introduce them to someone else and say it's Keisha so they can get off your case."

Adrian looked at Melanie with confused plastered across his face. "What the hell are you talking about, that sounds like some crazy kid shit!"

"It just may be crazy enough to work," Melanie said as smiled and took another sip of her drink.

"Okay, fuck it, I'll play. So... how am I going to find a female to go along with this whole story?"

"You're looking right at her."

"Seriously, you'd do that for me. And what would you want in return?"

"Some dick," Melanie said nervously. She knew she was putting herself on the line by saying this. But she had a master plan and she knew she had to play dirty to get what she wants. Her new plan was to get with Adrian, fuck it, Keisha just wasn't the one for him.

Adrian couldn't believe what he just heard, and there was no way he was going to ask her to repeat herself. As soon as she said that, he pictured himself fucking Melanie. He knew she wanted something else from him, but he is still a weak man when it comes to pussy. "I think that can be arranged, but what about my brother?"

"Don't worry about it, I'll handle that. I'll just make up some bullshit like I just came out on this date to help Keisha out and let him know I already have a boyfriend or some shit."

"Wow, you're really good at lying to people. I think you're kind of crazy, but I kind of like it."

"Good. So when can I get some dick. My pussy is getting wet just thinking about your sexy caramel inside of me."

"Whenever is fine with me. This shit is crazy," Adrian said smiling. It's been a while since he had any drama or excitement in his life. But he felt a small tinge in his heart when the thought about how this would hurt Keisha if she found out. But he soon got over his fear as he felt the side of Melanie stiletto going up the side of his pants as he looked down at her busty cleavage.

## Chapter VII: Bros before Hoe's

Keisha woke up to the smell of bacon and soon after heard the sound of sizzling bacon as her vision cleared and she realized she was in her parents' house. She felt so blessed that a lot of things in her apartment could be salvaged. She was also thankful that Mr. Wiggles made it out okay, despite all the smoke from the fire of the apartment next to them; she knew it was a miracle and was happy the firemen got there in time to put out the fire. She knew what she had to do now, she had to begin looking for a new place—she wouldn't be able to stay at her parents for long because they would be all up in her business. Her mom had already questioned her for hours about where she was the night the fire happened; Keisha wasn't ready to tell her mom about her new boyfriend, especially because of his profession. Of course her mom wanted the best for her, but she would freak out and not understand why she would want to date a ball player—she already knew the speech her mom would give her; her mom would talk about how ball players are cheaters and how she needs to find someone that is more serious about her.

"Are you hungry Keisha?" asked Mrs. Patterson as she walked into her guest bedroom and began picking up Keisha's clothes from last night off the floor and folding them. She was startled as Mr. Wiggles came and tugged on Keisha's shirt with his teeth, thinking she was in the mood to play. "Keisha, get this damn dog before I kill it!" Mrs. Patterson yelled as she snatched the shirt from Mr. Wiggle's mouth.

"Come here Mr. Wiggles," Keisha said as she giggled about what just happened. Her mom hated dogs, so she knew her stay there wouldn't last very long.

"I made bacon, eggs, and pancakes."

"Okay, I'll be down, thanks mom," Keisha said as she relentlessly climbed out of the comfortable queen sized bed. She wanted to sleep in, but she knew that there was a ton to do today. She needed to look for apartments and call Melanie to see what happened last night at Daniel's restaurant after she had to leave. She was kind of upset that Melanie didn't call her to check on her, but she figured Adrian must of told her she was okay; but she knew Melanie was selfish and she didn't feel like fighting with her.

"Thanks mom, breakfast was bomb," Keisha said as she brought her plate over to the sink.

"You're welcome sweetie. So, what do you have planned today?"

"Nothing crazy, just looking for a new place and I have a few errands to run. Mr. Cook said I won't be able to get any of my stuff out of the building until all the smoke started to settle. So I need to buy a few new outfits, toiletries, and see if my clients scheduled for this week will allow me to come to them."

"You're such a busy bee, but I'm happy you're happy. You need to get a man. That will make you even happier, way happier than that stupid dog."

"Mom, I'm working on it. But that's the furthest thing from my mind right now. I'm just trying to make it through this week and pray that next week will be better."

"I know baby. Do you want me to put your clothes in the washer? I know that's the only outfit you have right now? You can use one of my old shirts, but I don't think I have any bottoms for you to wear?"

"No that's okay. I'm just going to throw the dress from yesterday back on and head out to the mall while everyone I know should be at work."

"Good idea. Okay, I'll let you go. Let me know if you need anything."

"I will mom, thanks. I love you. Thanks for everything," Keisha said as she exited the kitchen. It was time to get her day started.

After the mall, Keisha headed home to get a shower and start looking for apartments online. She went downstairs to walk Mr. Wiggles and decided to give Melanie a call. She was very surprised she hadn't heard from her in all these hours. She called Melanie, then Adrian, and both their phones went to voicemail. *"Uggh,"* she thought to herself, *"what the hell are they doing."* She then heard her stomach growl and realized that she didn't feel like cooking over her mom's house, not only did she not have groceries, but her mom was very anal about how she ran her kitchen, she liked everything in its place and for it to be sparkling clean after every use. While she had Adrian on her mind, she came up with a great idea to go to Daniel's restaurant to show support; it was only fifteen minutes away from her parent's house.

On the drive over to the restaurant, Keisha hoped in her mind that this wouldn't be awkward. But she was sort of excited to get there so she can ask Daniel what he thought about Melanie. For all she knew, they may have hit it off when she left; though she doubted that, Melanie was acting like a total brat and she hoped she had come to her senses.

"Welcome back," Daniel said, he immediately recognized Keisha as she walked in.

"Thank you, how's everything going?" she said, it's like they'd known each other all their lives. She was relieved about how easy he was to talk to.

"Great! Thanks," Daniel said as he walked Keisha over to the bar to take her order.

"It looks like it. You already have some clientele," She complimented as she looked around and saw that the restaurant was halfway full.

"Indeed, I just hope it stays like this every day of the year."

"It will. Positive attitudes only, it's not easy being an entrepreneur. If it was, everyone would be one."

"I know that's right. If I listed to all the haters who said it wasn't possible I would still be working a 9-5 job and unhappy. But I'm happy I followed my dreams; even if the restaurant does fail, I will have zero regrets and a lot of lessons learned as I continue on to my next venture. Anyway, enough about me. What brings you in here besides the wonderful food, I heard that your house caught on fire last night."

"Something like that, the apartment next door caught on fire. So I'm staying with my parents for now. I was hungry so I came to eat and support a hard working black man."

"Hey, there's nothing wrong with that. Thanks, I appreciate it. And oh, I'm glad you're okay. Is all your stuff okay?"

"Yeah, I just have to wait a week before I can get some of my stuff, I'm looking for a new place. I saw a few potentials I have a meeting to see three spots tomorrow. I just wish I didn't have to move, although that building can get annoying, the rent was super low, and I love saving my coins!"

"That's right. When you find a place for a great price, keep it as long as you can."

"So, wassup with your friend? She seems more interested in my brother than she does in me?"

"What made you say that?"

"She didn't come over and say anything else to me for the rest of the night. She even left without saying goodbye. All she did was sit at that table and talk to Adrian. I know that he's your man and all, but you better keep an eye on her. I was watching her body language and she looks like she was looking for trouble."

"Yeah she's something else. She was probably talking him into introducing her to his friends. She's looking for a ball player I think. Which is fine, but I didn't want her to pressure Adrian into it. I have to call them."

"So I guess I'm not good enough for her?"

"That's not true. You're more than good enough, she just has her priorities and when she puts her mind to something she is very determined to get it. That's all."

"Well...I won't be playing football anytime soon, so I guess I should let that go. She's a very nice looking girl, I just wish she had a better personality, something sort of like yours."

Keisha blushed. "Aww, thanks. I try to treat people how I want to be treated. Adrian is lucky to have a brother like you."

"And Melanie is blessed to have a friend like you, because she sure as hell don't deserve it!"

They both laughed and spent hours talking about everything. Adrian, business, relationships, the whole nine. Keisha looked down at her watch and knew she should head back to her parent's place before her mom got nosy.

"Well it's been nice. Make sure to give me a call if you ever need anything."

"Thanks. I'll make sure to do that."

As Keisha left the restaurant, she couldn't help but wonder why she felt butterflies in her stomach when she talked to Daniel. She loved Adrian, but she and Daniel seemed to have connection on a much deeper level. She knew that she had to cut off all ties from

Daniel. There was no way she was going to let herself fall in love

with her boyfriend's brother.

# Chapter VIII: Mixing Drinks

"Wow... she's gorgeous. You should have been brought her around. Is she coming to next week's game?" asked Mike.

"I'll be there," Melanie said smiling. She could get used to all this attention. She hardly knew what to do with herself being around all these well-paid men. All she knew is she wanted to be a part of this lifestyle, and she didn't care who she had to hurt in order to get it.

"Sounds good. You know my boy Adrian here is a good catch. He really has matured and I'm proud that he's with you, because he just seems so much happier at practice. Just keep doing what you're doing," Mike said, patting Adrian on the back while smiling ear to ear. He is genuinely happy to see his friend happy all the time lately.

"Yes, this one is a keeper. I'll be sure to keep her around because she does make me happy," Adrian said thinking about Keisha, but looking sort of awkwardly at Melanie. He was beginning to feel bad about all these games, it was beginning to interfere with his sleep and his conscience. He didn't like lying to his friends, and to the world for that matter. He avoided thinking about what Keisha would think or do if she found out about this. He got a sharp pain in his gut, letting him know he was wrong. He wish he had thought about it more before going through with Melanie's crazy plan.

"Aww, that's so sweet, he makes me happy too," Melanie proclaimed, feeling nothing but ecstasy. She thought Adrian sounded genuine. She had to continue getting into his head until he was her man in real life. At first she wanted to get close to other ball players through Adrian, now she was beginning to think Adrian is the one she would go after.

Adrian began to take Melanie around to his meet his other team members before practice started. They all pretty much had the same reaction; the commented on how beautiful she was and wanted to see more of her. He then saw Melanie off and ran back in the stadium to start practice. He couldn't believe himself, he felt bad but he also felt a sense of relief. Now he didn't have to keep getting questions from his team mates and friends about meeting his new girl. Ever since he announced that he was in a new relationship, it seemed like everyone wanted to meet this "dream girl" that was making him so happy and making him a better man. His friends saw changes in him; good changes, like more patience, more respect when discussing women, and he just seemed like a happier person all around. But Adrian would never get over the fact that it wasn't Melanie, but Keisha who is the real reason behind his change in behavior.

As Adrian put his practice jersey over his shoulder pads, he saw his phone lighting up and vibrating. It was a text from Melanie saying how she wanted to meet up later that night. He wasn't sure what he wanted to do just yet, so he ignored the text, and finished getting dressed and put his phone in his locker; secretly hoping that locking it away would keep all this drama he had created from forming. He hated the feeling of having to hide something all the time, and he wished he had confidence like Keisha to face the world not caring what others think. He got a spark of inspiration inside of him and promised himself inside his head that he would never let Keisha find out about this, he needed to protect her heart no matter what. He would meet up with Melanie later tonight in order to tell her that they can continue pretending to go out to keep up the facade for his friends, but they would not be seeing each other in private.

Melanie got the text from Adrian letting her know it was okay to stop by, her face lit up when she saw his address pop up on her screen. *"This is it; I have to be on my A game tonight."* She thought to herself. Melanie had plans to seduce Adrian tonight, she knew he would come to his senses about dating Keisha. Obviously he needs a real woman in his life, one that can actually be shown off in front of his friends and family. Having someone like Keisha around was just not good for his career because he is obviously too embarrassed to show her off. But messing with a bad bitch like Melanie is what's acceptable. Melanie knows she's irresistible, so she pulls out one of her sexiest dresses that shows a ton of cleavage and a lot of leg and some high heels to seal the deal. She looks in her full length mirror and admires the body she works so diligently to maintain. She rubs her freshly manicured nails down the sides of her body paying close attention to her petite hour glass figure. While moving her long wavy hair to the side as she takes a quick glance at her butterfly tattoo that gives her light skin a look of creativity and expression. While pushing up her boobs one more time to make sure they look perky and large, she looks at the clock and sees that she needs to get going.

As Melanie pulls up to the gated community and is buzzed in; she can tell that she hit the jackpot. Her GPS guides her as she strolls pass huge houses like the ones that she's only seen on TV. She always pictured herself living the lavish lifestyle, and has detailed plans of Adrian being her meal ticket. As she pulls up to his driveway, she smiles as she looks at his huge mansion-like house and three flashy cars sitting in the driveway. The porch light comes on as she walks up his stairs feeling sexy in her heels, she rings the doorbell. Her heart begins to beat faster as she stands on Adrian's porch in the middle of the night dressed up and ready to be his one and only.

"Come on in," Adrian says, "this won't be long, I just want to go over a few things." Melanie steps into the big glamourous house very impressed by its interior design. She doesn't even notice that Adrian has invited her to have a seat in the living room because she's so distracted with all the fancy stuff. "Melanie?" Adrian calls out to her again, just noticing how sexy she was looking.

"Oh yes, sorry, thanks for inviting me over," she says, slowly taking a seat right beside him on the couch.

"No problem. First, I just wanted to thank you for doing that for me. I know it wasn't easy."

"It was my pleasure. I had a blast."

"That's good. I do need you to continue to come to the games, but I just want to make sure we're on the same page."

"I'm sure we are," Melanie says as she gently rests her hand on Adrian's thigh while looking him right in the eyes.

Adrian immediately feels his manhood rise and can't help but look down Melanie's dress at her perky breasts. "Let me get us something to drink," he says, trying to escape the situation. He can already tell that she came here to seduce him. He goes into living room and takes a bottle of wine off the rack and begins to prepare two glasses while trying to get his mind focused on letting Melanie know that Keisha can't find out about them. He returns with the two glasses and has a seat back on his black leather sofa beside Melanie.

"Look, Keisha can't know anything about this. I don't want to hurt her," he says as he hands Melanie her glass.

"I'm not thinking about Keisha right now," Melanie says, scooting closer to Adrian and placing her hand back on his thigh.

He wants to respond but before he can she leans over and begins to kiss him. He can't help but indulge himself. He can taste the sweet red wine on her pretty pink lips as he gently bites her bottom lip. Melanie saddles him and begins to unbuckle his belt, revealing his rock hard cock and slides in into her already wet pussy. She moans as she bounces up and down riding his cock, Adrian puts his hands on her waist guiding and encouraging her to continue going. He puts his head back in ecstasy as he feels her gentle wet walls surrounding his manhood. While riding his cock, Melanie pulls out her breasts and reveals her hard nipples. "You like that daddy?" she says as she begins to grind harder on his dick. "Yes baby, don't stop," he says as he enjoys her. His cum releases into her as she slows down her hips and gives him a gentle kiss on the lips.

Adrian can't believe what just happened, he thought he had more willpower than this. There was no way he could set boundaries with this woman or even have a talk with her tonight after what just happened. He continues to think about Keisha and how his dreams of being with her seems to be pushed further back into the distance with every choice he makes.

# Chapter IX: Dirtying Up The Kitchen

"You've been here every day this week, you must love the food here huh?" Daniel asked Keisha, teasing her as usual. He walked over to her table to see how she was doing.

"The food is amazing. I'm just happy to get a break from my mom any chance I get. This all reminds me of why I moved out in the first place. I love her but she can be overbearing," Keisha replied, realizing how close her and Daniel were becoming. Ever since the grand opening, her and Adrian have only been talking once a day on the phone, they used to talk all the time. It's like every time she wants to meet up he claims he's busy so she only got to see him twice this week.

"I know what you mean, you're always welcome here."

"Thanks, I appreciate that."

"So anyway... how's my brother doing?"

"Okay I guess, we've been talking less, but I just went over his house last night. It was nice, but it seems like he's going through something... he's been distant lately," Keisha said, hoping that she didn't overstep her boundaries by exposing their problems to Adrian's brother.

"Going through something, huh, I'll give him a call and see what's on his mind. We're not as close as we used to be. I mean, we still support each other and go to each other's stuff, but I've been so busy over the last year getting this restaurant together that I didn't have time for anyone really. I really need to be there for him more."

"Yeah I feel you, sometimes you have to do what you have to do in order to make your dreams come true. If I chose back then to go out with my friends instead of searching for ways to get new customers and retaining the ones I had instead, I probably wouldn't be where I am today either. It's one of those things where you can't feel guilty, because you only get one life and you have to make choices, everyone may not agree or enjoy, but sacrifice is the ultimate price for success."

"I'll drink to that!" Daniel said laughing, he couldn't believe how amazing of a woman Keisha is. He wished he found someone like her before Adrian did.

"Yeah, it can be lonely at the top."

"Indeed it can, so... has Adrian taken you to the Forbidden River yet?"

Keisha giggled a little because the name sounded so funny. She wrinkled up her face and asked, "What the heck is the Forbidden River?"

"It's only the most awesome view of the river from the city. I'm surprised you haven't gone since you've lived here so long."

"No I haven't, but it seems like fun."

"We should go. There's supposed to be a band playing there tonight. I'll call Adrian and we can head out there later on, I'm surprised he didn't take you."

"Okay, sounds like a plan. Like I said, he's been so "busy" lately."

While putting on her makeup in the mirror, Keisha spanked Mr.

Wiggles on his butt for pooping in her mom's closet earlier. She

had to get out of this house, she believed Mr. Wiggles could tell her

mom didn't care for him. She ran the flat iron through her hair, and

put the final touches of blush on her right cheek, when she saw her

phone light up on her dresser. Her pink glittery nail swiped across

her glass screen so she could view the message she just got from

Adrian letting her know he wouldn't be able to make it to the

Forbidden River tonight. She put her head down in disappointment,

she couldn't believe he was bailing at the last minute. Just as she

lifted her head to look in the mirror, her phone began to ring, it

was Daniel. He still wanted to go so she decided to tag along, she

was already dressed in one of her favorite blue jean dresses

anyway. There was no reason to waste a perfectly good outfit.


Keisha plugged the address into her GPS and made her way over to

the Forbidden River, there was no way that she was going to let

Daniel pick her up from the house like he insisted because she

didn't want her mom all up in her business. As she pulled up, she saw lots of families enjoying a nice day at the park, most of the park benches were taken but she saw people packing up, it was about to get dark, and plus it was a week day and people most likely had to get ready for work in the A.M. She got out the car, not sure where she should park, and began walking over to a reservoir-like body of water. She looked out into the water and smiled as she saw a baby geese following their mother in the pond. It was so cute. Startled by a light touch on her shoulder, Keisha turned around to see Daniel smiling at her. Her heart jumped for a second, and she couldn't help but smile ear to ear, she had no idea she'd be so excited to see him.

"I'm glad at least two of us could make it," Daniel said sarcastically.

"I know. Adrian has been bailing a lot lately, I hope he's okay," replied Keisha, nudging Daniel to inform her if he knew anything more than what she knew.

"He's always been like that, not really the committed type. Seems to bail last minute, I guess he gets distracted easily."

"Well… that's not good," Keisha said, chuckling a little bit.

"Sometimes we have to take the good with the bad. But anyway, let's talk about how awesome this band is going to be."

Keisha and Daniel continued to talk about the band, relationships, and life in general. They both enjoyed the same R&B music and was a believer in having a soul mate. As they continued to talk, Keisha could feel herself letting go of her insecurities, it was like talking to a really good friend that she knew for years. It stumped her that she and Daniel had such a great connection. Keisha held their spots on the lawn as the band began to set up for the show, Daniel came jogging over with two lawn chairs that he had in the back of his trunk. They enjoyed some great music, and now it was time to head home.

"I had an amazing time tonight, you sure know some good music, thanks for the invite," Keisha said.

"It was my pleasure, I have to put you on what goes on around this town. You been her longer than me and you don't even know where the hot spots are," Daniel teased.

"I know, I've always been a homebody. But I'm starting to get out more, and I'm loving it. Especially now that I don't have a 9-5 to worry about."

"I know that's right! So anyway, you have a good night. And make sure you hit me up if you need anything."

"Thanks, I'll do that."

Daniel embraced Keisha and she couldn't help but get a naughty tingle in her box. She felt a little bad, but she figured it was normal when hugging fine black men. She stepped back, feeling relieved that it was dark because she didn't want Daniel to see that her nipples were hard. As Keisha headed home, all she could think about is how much fun she had tonight. He really knew how to party and she loved his entrepreneurial spirit that complimented hers. Her phone vibrated and lit up as she stopped at a red light, it was a text from Daniel. *"I had a really great time tonight, we have to do something again soon."* Keisha couldn't believe he was asking her out again, she felt butterflies in her stomach but at the same time she felt sort of weird that he was so direct, being that she was dating his brother and all. The porch light came on and gnats surrounded it as Keisha rumbled through her purse to find the key to her mom's house, she finally go in, went up the stairs and into the guest room and plopped on the bed. As she got naked and stepped into the shower, her mind still pondered rather she should see Daniel again, she didn't want any trouble. Keisha being the loyal person that she is, made a commitment to herself that she would no longer be involved with Daniel; that meant no more trips to the restaurants, etc. She found a good man in Adrian, and she would not mess it up. She knew she'd be stepping into the danger zone if she pursed this relationship any further. As she drifted off to sleep, she felt a little better about the situation because she knew where her loyalty lied.

"So how'd it go last night? The band tore it up didn't they?" Adrian asked Keisha, happy that she was getting along with her brother. The only thing was, he didn't want Daniel to spill the beans about him messing around with Melanie; that's why he's been trying to keep them both at a distance.

"It was great, I had a lot of fun. Your brother is something else," Keisha responded, happy that Adrian decided to give her a call on this beautiful Friday morning.

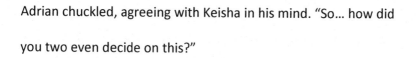

Adrian chuckled, agreeing with Keisha in his mind. "So... how did you two even decide on this?"

"You know I'm at my mom's place so I've been eating at his restaurant, just to give him some support and to get out the house and get some decent food."

"Ah... okay."

"Yeah, but I actually have an apartment viewing today, I'm about to just move in anywhere because I don't think I can stay here much longer."

"Yeah I hear you."

"So when is your next game, I really want to go to one."

"I'm not sure, but I'll definitely get back to you when I can get you some tickets. They've been stingy with the tickets, I guess budget cuts."

"Wow that's crazy, there's always something."

"Yeah, but I definitely want you to meet my friends. They've been asking about you."

"I'd like that. Speaking of your friends, I don't think my friend Melanie is interested in your brother. I think she wants a ball player, I haven't talked to her in a while but I'm sure she would like to meet them as well."

"I'll see what I can do."

"Thanks, I know it's a lot to ask, but she's a really good friend and even though she can be a pain in the ass at times, I'm still always there for her."

"Yeah I know what you mean."

While driving over to the apartment complex that Keisha was thinking about moving into, she couldn't help but wonder why Melanie has been missing in action for the month. She hadn't spoken with her since the grand opening and she was starting to get concerned. The only thing Melanie did was respond back to her text messages occasionally. After the meeting, Keisha decided to stop by and see her but when she pulled up to her place, her car wasn't there. Worried and sort of annoyed, Keisha left Melanie a note on her door letting her know she was trying to reach her. *"No telling what this girl has gotten herself into, she must have found a man,"* Keisha thought to herself. Usually when Melanie gets a boyfriend, she would completely cut everyone else off. It was all about her and her man. She spent countless hours making sure everything in the relationship was going perfect, and working on her body. Keisha always got annoyed because she took it overboard. But Keisha had better things to worry about, she was about to move into a brand new apartment and she was super excited about it.

# Chapter X: We're Both Playing The Game

"I need to know why you still haven't invited to meet your friends, and you haven't even took me out anywhere since our first date. What's going on? I'm tired of coming over your house to see you," Keisha asked in the most polite voice she could, she was getting aggravated with Adrian. He always came up with an excuse to stay in the house. She was tired of going over his house to make love and then going back to her new apartment.

"I know babe just be patient with me I have a lot of my mind and things aren't as simple as you think, "Adrian pleaded. He just couldn't get around to telling Keisha the truth, he really needed to let her know that he was embarrassed, but he didn't want her to see him as weak. He also didn't want her to feel insecure about her body, because he really did love the way she looked and felt, but he knew other people may not necessarily agree. He felt more insecure than she did obviously, but his ego wouldn't allow him to admit it.

"Please just let me know what's going on, I'm a big girl, I can handle it."

"Nothing is wrong, I just need you to be patient with me. Like I said there's a lot going on, I don't want to talk about this right now."

"Well when can we talk because I hardly ever see you outside of four walls. Just be honest with me, honesty is key in a relationship and I feel like you're not open."

"I am open, just not to certain things…"

"Okay, now we're getting somewhere. What aren't you open with?"

"Um…"

"I think I know what's going on here. I just wanted you to admit

that it was true. I've always been confident in who I am and how I

look and I don't give a damn what people think of me because I

can't pay my bills with their opinions. There's no way I'm going to

let a simple thing like my weight keep me away from being happy.

So... is all this hiding at your house because you're embarrassed to

be seen with me in public, are you afraid that your friends will

make fun of you for being with me because of my weight?"


Silence filled the phone lines as Keisha patiently waited for an

answer. Adrian's heart began to beat radically, he was so surprised

and afraid of how well Keisha knew him. He still wasn't ready to

admit the obvious.


"Hello?" Keisha said, ensuring him that she was still on the other

end of the phone.

"Well… you said it, not me…" Adrian managed to say so low that Keisha could hardly hear him.

"Okay, so now that I know the problem. Let's work on the solution. I'm fine over here. I know what I want, I also know that you love me because of the way you treat me. So, what do you think we should do?" Keisha was trying to be patient with Adrian because she didn't want to put too much pressure on him. She figured he could come up with the solution, because he's the one who had the problem.

"All I know is there's no way I can introduce you to my friends, they're just assholes and I don't want to hurt you."

"But we can still go out and do stuff right?"

"I'm trying to avoid that because I may run into one of them, it's a small town."


"Wow! You're that worried? I mean I can see you not blatantly introducing me to them, but you don't even want to be caught out with me? Now that's a little bit too much. I really need to think about things. I'll give you a call back." Keisha hung up the phone feeling like her heart had just been torn out, she couldn't believe his audacity, she's smart as a whip and she knew there had to be more to the story. Because there was no way that he wouldn't even want to go out with her unless there was something else he was hiding. Keisha ignored her phone as it vibrated on the table with the screen lighting up saying "Adrian's calling". She didn't want to talk to him right now, it was time to put on her detective hat and go find out everything Adrian was too afraid to tell her. She got in her car and made her way over to Daniel's restaurant to do some digging.

"Hey pretty lady, I tried texting you the other night, wassup?" Daniel said, smiling, he was always happy to see Keisha. He had a feeling of relief when he saw her walking into the restaurant because he wasn't sure if she was avoiding him because of the connection they had the other night. He couldn't help but send her a text messages letting her know that he wanted to meet up again.

"A lot is up. Yeah I got your text, it's been crazy busy and on top of that your brother is acting crazy. But I really don't want to get into that right now. I just have a couple questions for you."

"Okay, shoot."

"Do you usually go to his games?"

"Hell yeah, I never miss a game. He always gets like six tickets to give out. Why? You haven't been to one yet?"

"No, because he told me that there were budget cuts so he couldn't get a lot of tickets."

"Aww mannnn...," Daniel said smiling and shaking his head. He didn't mean to smile but he couldn't help but get sucked into his brother's drama. He was just happy it wasn't him.

"Yup, so you know he's not doing right. So, when's the next game?"

"There's actually one tomorrow night. I'm surprised you didn't just look the schedule up online."

"I didn't look it up because I trusted what he was saying. I'm just messed up right now," Keisha said, too fed up to cry anymore. "I don't know what I'm gonna do."

"Well, I'm going to the game tomorrow and I would invite you with me, but obviously that's not a good look for my bro. He'll never forgive me. And plus, you don't want to go the game anyway to support him if you're mad at him."

"Yeah you're right," Daniel and Keisha continued to catch up. All Keisha could think about in the back of her mind was how she was going to buy her ticket and show up at that game. She had to see what the hell was going on. She didn't have time for the foolishness. A feeling of fear sat on Keisha stomach as she thought about how the encounter would play out if she actually ran into Adrian, or if Adrian found out she was there. She was never "that girl" to run around and stalk her man, but she had to do what she had to do.

"Thanks Daniel, it was nice talking to you. I'm sure we'll work things out," Keisha said as she left the restaurant, she immediately pulled out her phone as soon as the glass doors closed behind her. The ticket prices were not cheap being that it was a last minute purchase; but she purchased a ticket anyway, it was time to take action and get to the bottom of this once and for all.

As Keisha got dressed for the game, she had a sense of fear that wouldn't leave her alone. Her mind kept telling her to just forget it and not to take such a risk. She knew that by going to this game she'd be risking seeing Adrian and she wasn't sure how'd he react to it, all she knew was she wanted to see what was so special about these games that he had to hide from her.

She could hardly find parking, but she eventually parked her car on the higher level and took the shuttle over to the park. There were fans everywhere dressed in green and silver; rap music filled the entrance to the park as she handed the serious-looking security guard her purse and the representative her ticket. The hot sun hit her face as she went through the metal bars and looked at her ticket in order to find her seat. *"Hey thickness, how are you?"* a random guy shouted out to her. Even though she was used to this kind of attention it made her blush because she was nervous about running into Adrian or someone she knew. She wanted to be low-key, see what was going on, and haul her ass out of there. After walking around for fifteen minutes and looking up at the big numbers over the concrete openings of the stadium, she finally came across her section and walked over to take her seat. She felt at sense of relief as she went into her purse and took out her binoculars. That's right, she came prepared. As she caught her breath and looked around, she saw no one that she knew in sight, there was still fifteen minutes until the game started and she was hoping that it could stay like this. Popcorn flew out of the white guy with the big stomach's hand in front of her as cheered for the touchdown they just got. Keisha been spotted Adrian, but didn't get to see him play yet because he was on the bench. It seemed like an innocent game and Keisha began to let loose and enjoy it. After half time, the coach finally decided to put Adrian in and Keisha felt her heart drop as her man ran the field and played a great game. The game was finally over and the crowd jumped up and down and screamed, happy that their home team won the game. She watched intently as the players went back to the benches with huge smiles on their faces and began to celebrate with their family and friends who were sitting right behind them the whole time. Keisha smiled as she saw Adrian waiting there and looking at his phone, there seemed to be no one there for him. She felt bad, *"he must be texting Daniel,"* she thought to herself. Daniel told Keisha yesterday that he didn't have seats that close. She wished he Adrian told her he didn't have anyone, because she would have been there. She pictured herself giving Adrian a big hug and kiss after the game...when suddenly her heart dropped. Her eyes filled with disbelief as she saw Melanie go over to Daniel and give him a hug and passionate kiss on the lips.

"What the fuck?" Keisha said, her heart was beating out of her chest and she clinched her fists. There's no way this could be...

# Chapter XI: His Older Brother

It's been a whole week since Keisha talked to Adrian, she didn't tell him why she's been ignoring his call. She assumes Adrian believes that she is still upset over him being embarrassed of her. But that's not the case, she can't believe the terrible direction this relationship has started to go in, and all the sudden she sort of misses the days when she was single without a worry in the world. *"It's crazy when you ask God to send you something and he does, it's not always exactly what you pictured,"* Keisha thought. Keisha always wanted good man, she fantasized day and night that she'd meet a companion that will complete her. But she damn sure didn't ask to be lied to and cheated on; Keisha knew that Adrian has a good heart, she could tell. She always believes that he has good intentions, but it's obvious he has some growing up to do. While she's in deep thought about the turn her life has taken, Mr. Wiggle begins to bark at the top of his lungs as her phone vibrates on the shiny wooden kitchen counter. She surprised to see that it's a text from Daniel, *"I wonder what he wants, I sure as hell hope that Adrian didn't put him up to anything,"* Keisha thought as she gently slid her thumb across the glass face of her phone to look at the message.

"What are you doing tonight? There's Karaoke here at the restaurant and I'm trying to get a nice sized crowd, you should come out," Daniel's text read.

Keisha wasn't mad at Daniel because he's been nothing but nice to her, but she wasn't sure if she felt up to going out. And plus, she was afraid she might run into Adrian's lyin' cheating ass. She went on with her day, knocking two clients' heads out without a hitch. She was on the ball, and since she's been so productive, she did want to reward herself by going out. She finally texted Daniel back to see what time the event began and started choosing her outfit. Anger shot up through her body and burned her heart when the thought of the chance that she could see Melanie. Keisha didn't know what she would do if she saw that fake ass bitch. She was simply done with her and their friendship for good. Melanie hasn't

even called Keisha, so she knows she's shady. Keisha couldn't seem

to comprehend the audacity of Melanie, she couldn't believe that

her friend could stoop that low. She knew she was crazy and

selfish, but she didn't know she was a terrible person. Keisha put

on some R&B music to get the thoughts of fighting and anger from

her mind. She didn't think Adrian would go that far as to bring

Melanie along with him to an event like this. She figured he was

just using her as a prop to trick his friends in order to get their

approval. At the end of the day, Keisha didn't need this kind of

stress in her life; there were plenty of guys who tried to talk to her

on a daily basis, which appreciated her curves and her confidence.

But she continued to stick by Adrian, because they had an

undeniable connection. It's like ever since the day they met, she

could tell that he was the one. Every time she looked at him she

saw future memories of them being happily ever after, having

children, and having the big house with the picket fence, her

cooking him dinner, and them enjoying each other until they grew

up. She pictured them walking down the aisle and her writing their last name... *Mrs. Hartford*. She wasn't ready to give up these dreams and goals just yet. As badly as she hurt, she just wasn't ready.

Even if she hadn't supported Daniel, he would've been fine. The place was packed with people who came ready to party. Keisha strolled into the restaurant, looking fine as usual, with a white form fitting dress on. She smiled as she got smiles and compliments of men as she found a seat at the bar. Within minutes, she felt a stern hand on her shoulder and turned around to see it was Daniel. She got up to give him a hug.

"Thanks for coming out and supporting," Daniel said, smiling at Keisha while staring deeply into her brown eyes.

"Your welcome, it's my pleasure. Your events are always a blast," Keisha said, sort of blushing, but trying not to look away because she felt that would be awkward.

The night was a success. Keisha even got up on the stage and sang some Ashanti from back in the day. With drinks, meeting new people, and enjoying music, it was one of the most fun nights she had in a long time. She never wanted the night to end; she laughed as she thought to herself how foolish she was to let her and Adrian's situation linger in her mind for so long and take such a toll on her mentally, she did all that worrying and he didn't even show up tonight.

Keisha searched around to find Daniel to say goodbye before she left for the night.

"Thanks for everything! I had a blast," Keisha said, giving Daniel a big hug and putting her purse over her shoulder.

"Your welcome, I'm glad you can come out. You're really beautiful, you know that?"

Keisha was caught off guard, she didn't expect to hear that last part. She tried not to smile but she couldn't help it, it crept through and she blushed fiercely. "Thanks, that's really sweet," she said. Trying to find a reason to just get up and leave at the moment, she felt her heart lift and butterflies filled her stomach, she wasn't sure what her body was doing and she just wanted to leave. She felt awkward and didn't want Daniel to see that.

"You don't have to thank me, you're the one who's looking so good. So, how's my brother treating you?"

Keisha paused and thought for a second. She didn't' want to whine and scare Daniel off with her drama and sob stories. She just wanted to get out of the restaurant so she could have some time to herself to think about things. "Things could be better, but we're

working on it," she said, not wanting to get into details.

"The game the other day was great, they won. I'm surprised he

didn't invite you out."

"Yeah, I guess he's busy or whatever. But I need to get home—"

Daniel interrupted Keisha before she could come up with an excuse

of why she need to leave. "You don't have to be alone. I'm here to

listen, you should come over and we can crack open a bottle of

wine and talk about it. I can tell there's something on your mind."

"I don't know if that's such a great idea, I should get going."

"You know, you can't hide forever. Sometimes we all need that friend who we can confide in, and I doubt if Melanie would keep your secrets very well."

"Well… Okay, I guess I can have one glass. But I don't want to be out too late. I have a client tomorrow at 9 in the morning."

"I won't keep you too long, this will be your time to get some things off your chest. I only want to pay you back and support you from all the support you've given me, that's all."

All of this made sense in Keisha's mind. Daniel was simply trying to be a friend, and who was she to deny herself of friendship at a time like this. She felt comfortable as she left out to drive over to meet Daniel at his apartment. As she drove along the road with love songs playing on the radio, she thought what it would be like if she had met Daniel first before Adrian. She wondered what they'd be like together, she then shook her head furiously as if that would help the thoughts to escape. It is just wrong to date your boyfriend's brother.

His couch was so soft and fluffy, it felt like Keisha was seeping into it. As soon as she sat down on the beige cotton couch, it felt like she could sit there forever. Daniel returned into the well-lit room with a glass of red wine in each hand.

"Here you go," Daniel said as he extended his muscular arm to hand Keisha the glass, "So tell me what's bothering you."

Keisha giggled a little because it felt like she was in a therapy session. She didn't really know where to start. "Well, thank you for the wine and your hospitality," she said, "I guess what's bothering me is the fact that I know your brother is cheating on me with Melanie."

Daniel pauses, his mouth gaping open and his eyes wide. "Are you serious? How do you know?"

"I did some snooping and went to the game the other day. After the game I saw him give Melanie a hug and kiss on the field."

"...that's fucking crazy. I mean, I know my brother can be an asshole at times, but that's just low. And with that ratchet bitch, I just can't...."

"Yeah, she was supposed to be my best friend, but obviously not anymore. She hasn't even called me. She just disgusts me on so many levels."

"I am so sorry that is fucked up, so you two are over, right?"

"No, he doesn't even know I know. He thinks I'm mad at him though. The thing is… "Keisha sighed in embarrassment and disappointment, but she felt cleansed every time she shared what she was going through with Daniel, "he basically told me he was too embarrassed of me to introduce me to his friends because of my weight."

"Now he didn't!"

"Yes… so he thinks I'm mad at him for that, he doesn't even know I know that. I'm assuming he's using Melanie as beard to show off to his friends."

"This is fucking crazy. I mean, I knew you were going through some shit, but I didn't know things have gotten this bad. How are you dealing with it?"

"A lot of crying and a lot of thinking. I'm just tired, I just want Adrian and I to be together without all these outside circumstances. His "so called" friends and society are obviously putting pressure on him to only date a woman with certain looks."

"Are you serious? He can't use peer pressure as an excuse to cheat. I'm sorry but that's just bullshit, and I won't allow you to make excuses for a grown as man who can't even keep it real with himself or anyone for that matter."

Keisha bent over and began to sob into her hands, she knew damn well that Daniel was right. She was tired of making excuses, it was what it was. She hated that she was so weak and so willing to forgive him for what he's done. A gentle yet powerful hand touched her back, and a feeling of warmth tingled through her body.

"It's okay," Daniel said gently as he sat beside Keisha and continued to rub her back.

His deep masculine voice made her feel the most safe and secure she had ever felt in her life. She picked her head and Daniel wiped the tears from her eyes using the sides of his hands. The kiss they shared was slow and moist, Keisha's lips tingled with excitement, and she could feel her hard nipples protruding from her bra. She looked deep into his eyes, and her heart dropped as he stared back into hers and touched the side of her face gently. The moment was so beautiful that Keisha's eyes began to well up with tears again. Daniel slowly slid his hand down and cupped Keisha's large erect breast with his hands and began to kiss and suck on her neck gently. Keisha felt herself getting wet and moaned in delight, her heart beat fast as she got more and more turned on by his touch. He lifted the bottom of her dress up to her belly button to expose her black lace panties. Keisha excitedly opened her legs wide to give Daniel access to her goodies, his tongue slid inside her as she grabbed the back of his head to encourage him to keep licking her spot. Within minutes, Keisha was cumming all over his tongue and he was kissing on her clit making her squirm as he began to pull out his rock hard cock. As he slid inside of her, he felt her tight wet walls grasping his dick. He began to thrust in and out of her while pinching her chocolate nipples between his fingers. Keisha grabbed Daniel's ass he continued in and out of her and she pulled him in closer, she wanted his whole manhood inside of him. *"This feels so good, baby,"* Daniel whispered as he lifted Keisha's legs in front of him and continued to pump, this time he sped up and began to cum inside of her as he bit his bottom lip, trying to contain himself.

## Chapter XII: I Can't Keep Both of You

It's been three weeks and Daniel and Keisha have been inseparable. They hang out every night; it's like they were truly meant to be together. Daniel is excited and feels blessed to be having a sleepover every night with such a phenomenal woman; and Keisha feels bad that she feels so good. It's been so long since she took a call from Adrian, he's been trying to get in touch with her for weeks, but now she can't even be mad at him for what he did—because what she's done is way worse. She not only slept with his brother, but accidently fell in love with him. She tried many times in her mind to cut this off, she knows she's down bad, but she can't help but want this man. And he's such a good man too… *"Why does he have to be such a good man,"* Keisha thinks to herself as she pours a hot fresh cup of coffee and looks out her kitchen window. Their parents really did a good job with these boys, they have good hearts. Torn between two brothers, Keisha doesn't want to face reality. There's no way she's going to let Adrian find out. She has to find a way to cut this off, because

Adrian's the one she sees a future with, he's the one she met by fate. She has to get back right with him so that her life could get back on track, she is willing to forgive him now and hopefully Daniel can keep his mouth closed about the affair. This won't be easy, not because of her feelings for Daniel, but because of Daniels feeling for her. She doesn't want to hurt him, but she knows this can't go on for much longer.

Keisha walks into Daniel's restaurant right before closing time, tonight he would be taking her to a late night show and she wanted to help him clean up. As she squirts the chemicals onto the table and begins wiping it down, she hears a man's voice say:

"What the hell are you doing here?"

She turns and stands like a statue with her eyes wide as she watches Adrian walk over closer to her.

"So… what are you doing here? Do you work here now?" asks Adrian.

Keisha is just about to come up with a lame excuse when Daniel walks over to them and screams, "What's it to you? Where have you been?"

"What the hell is this?" Adrian screams in confusion.

"It's obvious, she doesn't want to be with you anymore. You go be with Melanie and let a real nigga take care of her."

Keisha is pushed against the wall as the two brothers begin fighting. Adrian is on top of Daniel punching him in the face when one of the cooks from the back comes out and breaks it up. She still can't believe this shit is happening.

"So, you fuckin' my girl?" Adrian yells to Daniel as his cook tries his back to hold him back.

"Just as good as you're fucking her best friend. I don't owe you anything man, you're a fuckin' snake. You don't every come to support the restaurant, you're cheating on Keisha, and you've always want to play the victim. I'm not doin' this tonight, man. I'm just not."

"Fuck you, you don't know what you're talking about," Adrian screams back at Daniel, "So is it true?" he turns and asks Keisha, "You're really fucking my brother?"

"I'm sorry," Keisha manages to say as she begins to cry.

"Yeah you are sorry!" Adrian yells as he turns away to leave. Before he can get out the door, he hears Keisha yell back:

"But you're fucking my best friend. And you've been doing it for months now."

"Yeah, but I'm not fucking your sister" says Adrian, walking back toward her.

"But she was like my sister."

"That's no excuse."

"You need to own up to how you've played a role in how this relationship went left. I was a good girl to you until you fucked up, never introduced me to your friends or invited me to a game, don't you dare pretend like you're innocent in this. There's no way I'm going to sit around and hide while you enjoy life because you're too much of a bitch to handle all of this!"

"Whatever. There's no moving forward from here. I'm done with you," Adrian yells back to his brother who is still being held back, "and I'm done with you too. You two deserve each other."

Too much time has passed and Keisha still hasn't heard from Adrian, she did not want him to find out the way he did, and she just can't get over that night. It keeps replaying in her head, and she just wants it to stop and clear her conscience. *"If he would just let me apologize, we could start working things out,"* Keisha thinks to herself. She's mentally exhausted and just wants to sit down with him and talk, they both need to apologize so they can move on. She has completely stopped talking to Daniel, she stopped answering his calls. She wants nothing else to do with him, because now when she thinks back, she can tell that Daniel had been trying to lure her in for a long time, inviting her to things and trying to get her alone. She didn't know if he did that because he actually liked her, or because he cared about her. Right now she didn't know who to trust and she just wants to make it right with the one she loves, Adrian.

"What are you doing out here?" Adrian says as he walks in his grey robe to get the mail.

"I'm sorry, I know this looks crazy but we need to talk," Keisha said, hoping he'll hear her out.

"Come in."

As she enters his home, she plays back the memories of the first time they made love in her head. She takes a set on his leather sofa, her hands intertwined, hoping that she could say the right words to get through to him.

"I was wrong and I apologize for what I did. You were right, what I did was far worse than what you did. And if you can find it in your heart to forgive me, I can forgive you as well," Keisha heart beats out of her chest as she waits for Adrian's reply.

"My brother can be something else. Him and I are back on good terms, and he let me know that it was him who started all this mess. He just didn't understand how I could treat a great girl like you the way I did and he wanted you all to himself. Although I'm still pissed, and very bothered by it; I guess I'm able to forgive you. But as far as a relationship goes... we'll have to see about that. I thought I was ready, but maybe I'm not..."

"That's all I want, is for you and I to be on great terms. And it means the world to me that you're willing to accept my apology."

Adrian gets up and goes over to the sofa to give Keisha a hug. As they embrace, he still believes she's the one for him, but he doesn't know if he can trust her anymore. But he knows one thing for sure, he doesn't want to lose her again.

## Chapter XIII: Three Can Play That Game

"I can't believe ya'll two fools are still together," Daniel said as he

brings in the salad and puts it in the middle of the dinner table,

"Well I'm not mad at ya'll, you're a lucky man Adrian."

Daniel has Adrian and Keisha over for dinner tonight at his place.

Keisha hadn't seen Daniel for a while and Adrian thought it would

be a good idea for them all to sit down and mend things. Keisha

hated the idea of it, but she had not place to argue.

"Yeah, it's been a rocky road, but we're on much better terms now.

All the stuff we went through has been crazy, but honestly I have to

thank you bro, because without you, I wouldn't have realized how

lucky I am," Adrian said, smiling and raising his glass of wine to the

ceiling.

"I guess," Daniel said, as he went back in the kitchen to check on the roast in the oven.

"So what's on the agenda for tonight," Keisha asked Adrian, trying her best to break the awkward silence.

"I'm not sure, I'm not the one hosting. All I know is I want to get drunk and have some fun," said Adrian, still high from the fact that he had a great football season.

"Same here," Daniel said, as he poured himself some dark liquor. "I'm going to get so drunk that I don't even remember this night."

"Now there, there, big brother, tonight is important and we shall treat it as such," said Adrian, already slurring his words.

Keisha didn't want to be the only one sober, so she poured herself another glass of wine as well. She was super nervous around Daniel. But at the same time, she didn't want to act funny around him.

"You're a very lucky man, I'm happy because we're closer than we've ever been. Just make sure to treat her like a queen," Daniel blurted out.

"Will do brother, will do. I don't want you two to think you can't be friends, I just don't want you two to be alone, if you know what I mean," said Adrian.

"I can't promise that," Daniel joked, "she's irresistible. How do your friends like her?"

"Dude, they love her. I just wish I had showed her off earlier, now I feel stupid and all of this could have been avoided. But I guess God wanted me to learn something from this," Adrian responded.

Keisha stayed quiet, she only felt comfortable talking if she was called on.

"Yeah I feel you. But I admit. I do miss it though, you know, the way Keisha used to give it to me," said Daniel.

"Give it one last go," Adrian said in a drunken slur, "Hurry up before I change my mind."

At this point Keisha was afraid because she didn't know what the hell was going on. Before she knew it Daniel was standing in front of her and knelt down to kiss her in the mouth. He then began to grab her waist and lick her neck slowly. Keisha was shocked, but turned on that Adrian would let this go down. She climbed on the dining room table and began to unbuckle Daniel's belt. His hard cock stood at attention as she put her warm lips around it and started sucking him off. Adrian came up behind her and lifted her dress over her plump ass and thrusted his manhood into her. Keisha tried her best to focus on sucking Daniels dick as Adrian grabbed her waist and continued plowing in and out of her. Daniel took his hands and went into the front of Keisha's dress, he put his head back in ecstasy as he began to pinch both of her erect nipples. Adrian then laid Keisha flat of the table and put his dick in her mouth as Daniel began to eat Keisha's wet juicy box. Daniel then stood up and put his dick in Keisha and thrusted in and out of her, groaning with pleasure. Keisha continued to slobber and suck Adrian's dick as he held the back of her head make sure she was hitting all the right spots. Adrian yelled, *"fuck"*, as he came in her mouth, and soon after Daniel began to tense up and shake as he came inside of her.

Two weeks later, Keisha woke up next to Adrian smiling. She loved her life. Everyone was on good terms, and things were beginning to get back to normal. Adrian had already warned her that the three-some was a onetime thing and that it's never happen again. He was drunk off his ass and he could hardly remember what happened. Keisha is okay with that, that night was super fun and it will always be in her memories. She thought it was a precious moment in time and she amazing sharing herself with the two men she loved most. Keisha threw her tired body out of bed and walked over to the bathroom so she could start her day when she felt the sickness again. She immediately ran over to the toilet to throw up. She had no idea what was going on with her body lately. All she knew is her breasts have been tender and she's been having morning sickness, she knew there was no way she could be pregnant because she took birth control pills.

After the appointment with her doctor, she found out that she was indeed pregnant. She hadn't been taking the pills as consistently as she should have. Keisha had no idea what she was going to do. She was afraid to tell Adrian because of the crazy night all three of them had together. It was a possibility that the baby could be Daniels. This scared the shit out of her. The sun danced across Keisha's face as she drove up to Adrian's house and got out of the car. As she put the keys in the tumbler, she had no idea how she was going to tell him she was expecting.

## Preview of "My Ex Does It Best"

*Chapter 1: Beginnings in My Bedroom*

As a married woman I still can't seem to get over him. I'm mean, I just can't up and erase these memories we've made. All the love making, the fights, the romance... it's something you just can't put an end to just like that. Call me crazy but I'm convinced that the only way to get over this man is to have that one last shot at our relationship. But who am I kidding? He has a kid now and a new girl. And I'm married to my husband, who is a good man—but the question still stands: is he really the one for me?

Shoot, before I get ahead of myself let me start from the beginning. I was in art class talking to my friend Lakeisha. I always told her the dirt I was up to, I was something else; I told her about all my dudes and what I was going through in relationships. I was a hot ass to be only 14 years old in high school. I had already dated two guys by time I even met

Jerome. But I played it cool, I played everyone when I think about it. Everyone thought I was the nerdy girl, the teacher's pet, and the goody two shoes. And I was... but not when it came to boys. I was boy crazy! But I did get good grades and go to school on time every day; a lot of people thought I was weird. Probably because I wasn't as hood as the others.

I grew up in an upper middle class family, but of course I still attended public school. So I had a lot of opportunities that others didn't; including Jerome. But I still loved me a hood nigga. I just couldn't get enough of the swag. Although most of my boyfriends were from the lower class neighborhoods, I never looked at that. We were just kids in high school, and the way I was holdin' it down I knew I could train any man to do what I wanted. I was the sweet little girl that didn't want any trouble.

All the other students knew that I was dating guys. They sure weren't afraid to hold anything back. I remember when a guy Malcom said "Dang, you have a lot of boyfriends."

Well, he was sort of right. I didn't keep my relationships very secret back then. I was pretty open to holding hands in the hallways and twerking on my man at school dances. So it was pretty much known all around school who I was dating at a particular time. By God's grace, I never got labeled as a hoe though. I only had one boyfriend at a time, so it couldn't be that bad.

My first boyfriend was Tyreek. He was definitely a hood dude. You couldn't tell him anything. He kept to himself in class. I got introduced to him through my friend Lakeisha.

I knew Lakeisha from middle school, so we had always been cool. Honestly, I liked being around her because she made me look like a ten! She was a very sloppy built girl, not very pretty in the face, but not hideous. She was about 60 pounds overweight and had bad acne. But that didn't stop her from getting dudes. Believe it or not, she was a hoe. Guys actually hit that, but only few would claim her. So that goes to show how nasty men can be, they just don't care.

**Visit www.SilkSheetBooks.com to continue reading My Ex Does It Best**

## Your Feedback Is A Gift!

Thank you again for reading *Giving Him More To Love*!

If you enjoyed this book, then I'd like to ask you for a favor, would you be kind enough to leave a review for this book on Amazon? It'd be greatly appreciated!

# Other Silk Sheet Books

To check out other silk sheet books visit www.SilkSheetBooks.com and to see other works by Shaneeka Porter, please visit her author page.

## My Ex Does It Best (5 Part Series)

## Romantic Island Getaway (4 Part Series)

# FREE BOOKS! *Remembering Him & Arousing Him*

CPSIA information can be obtained
at www.ICGtesting.com
Printed in the USA
LVOW01s1743170616

493067LV00025B/663/P